One day,
a very rough day,
he fell in.

The wind was **wild**.

The waves were **enormous!**

Teacup in a Storm

Written by
Lucy M George

Illustrated by
Il Sung Na

He was only little.

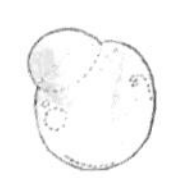

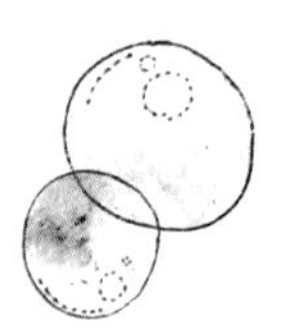

Then a friend appeared.

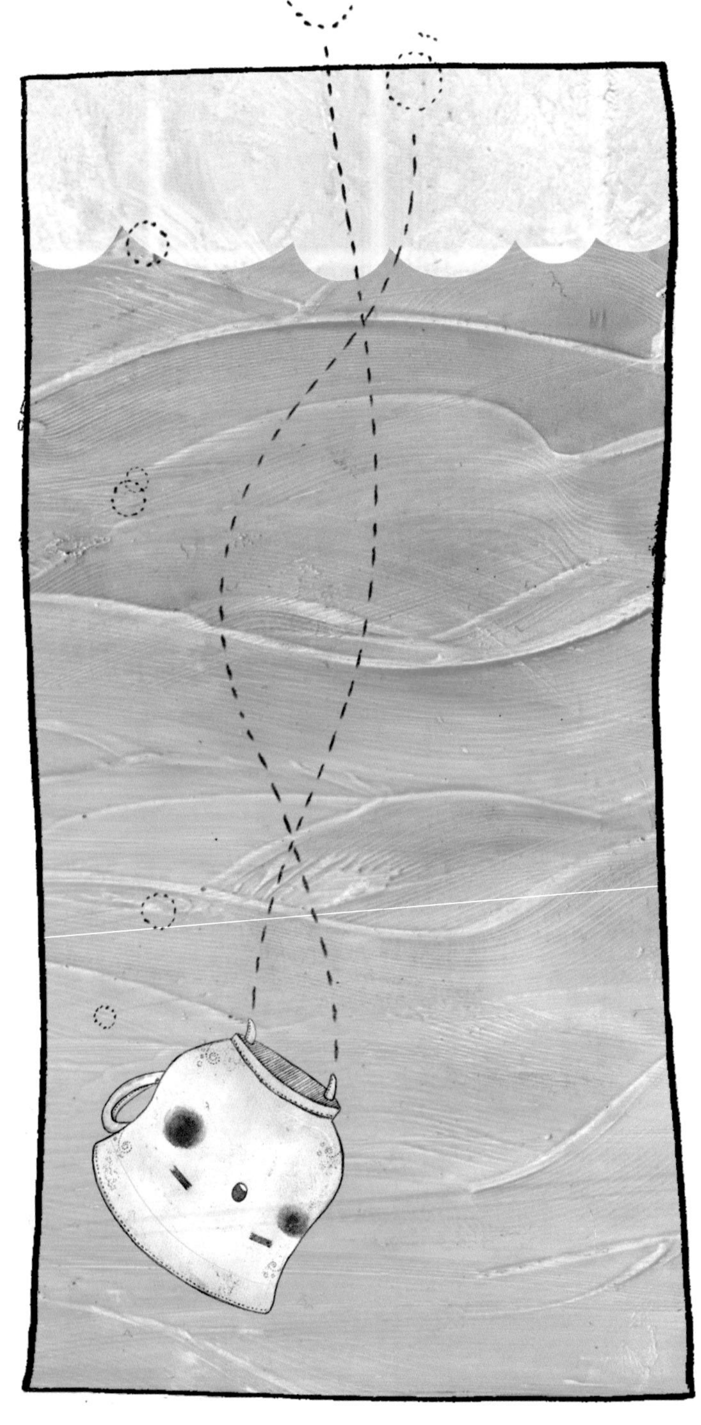

Hurray!

They went on a very long voyage together.

Through the **stormy** seas they sailed.

On wild and foaming waves they rode.

They went practically right around the world.

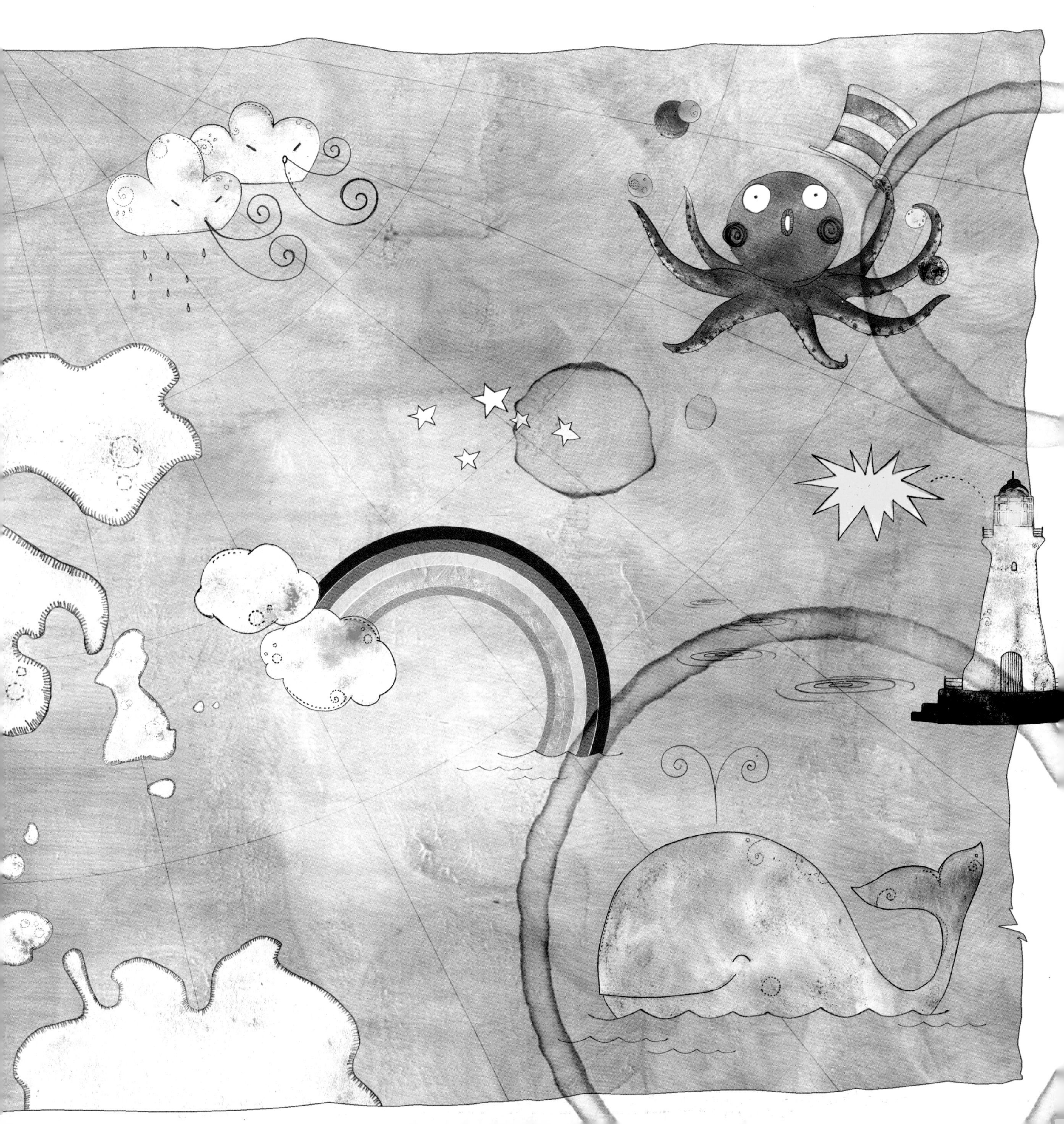

They saw **wonderful** things.

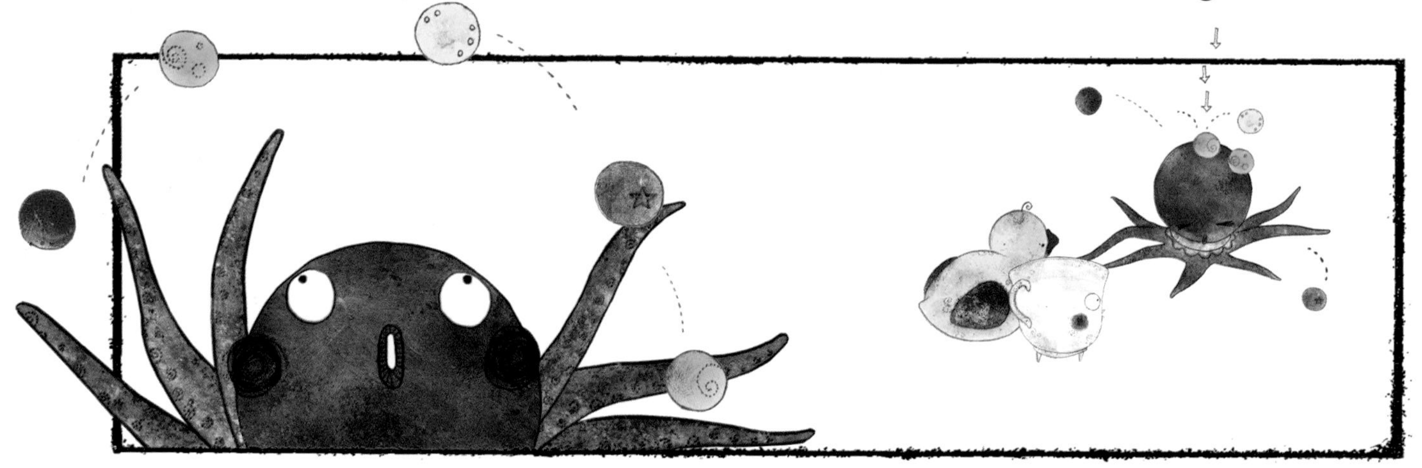

Funny things, **scary** things,

big **fat** hairy things!

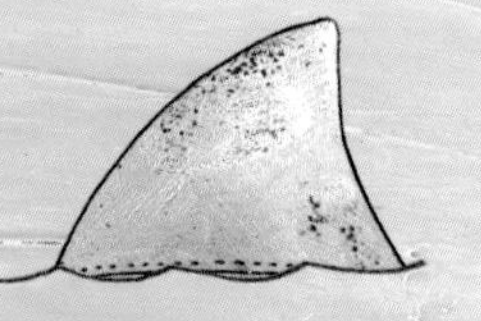

They held on tight,

(they were a little scared at night).

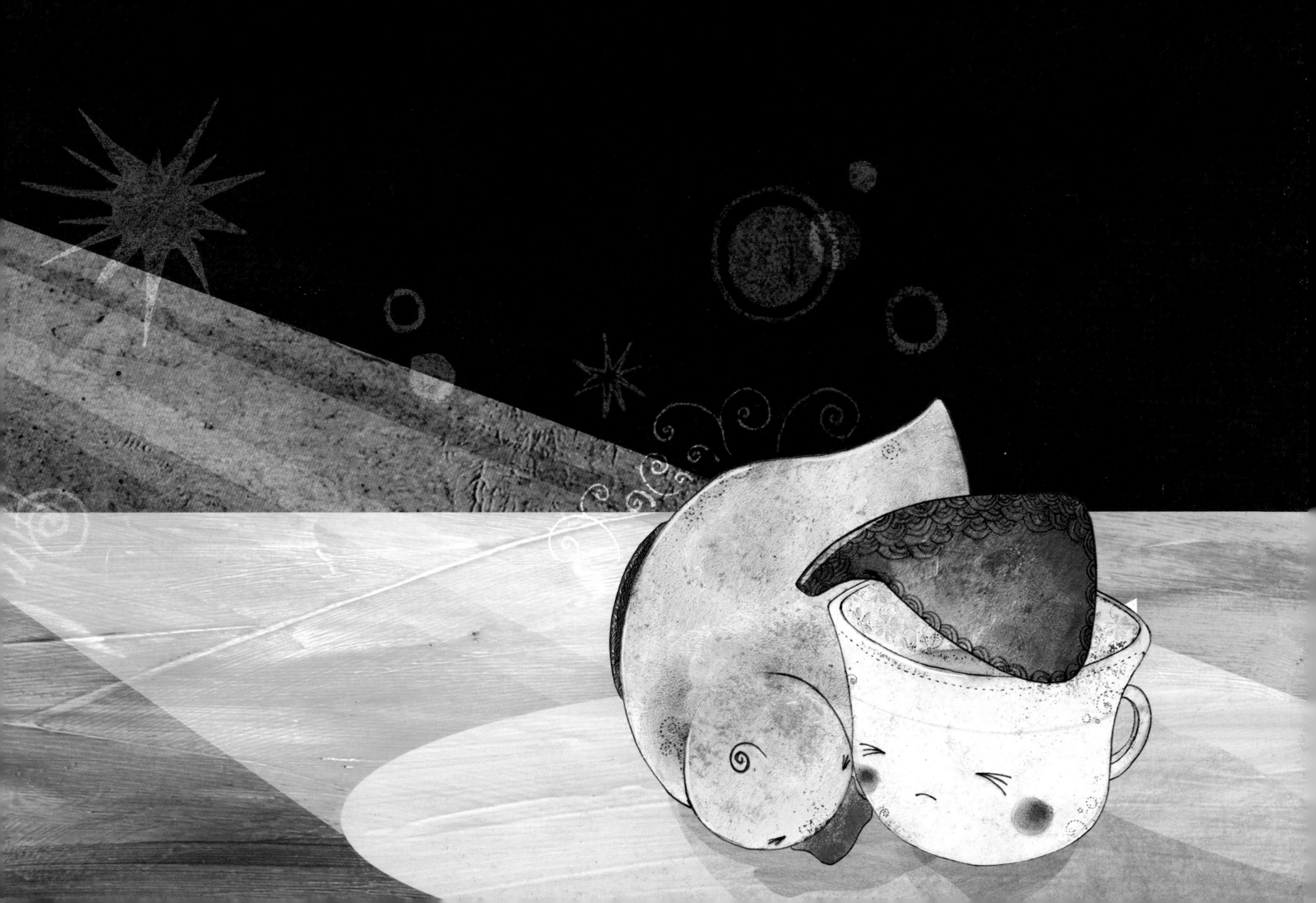

And then, after a
very long time...

the waves seemed
to get smaller.

Yes, they did!

They got smaller.

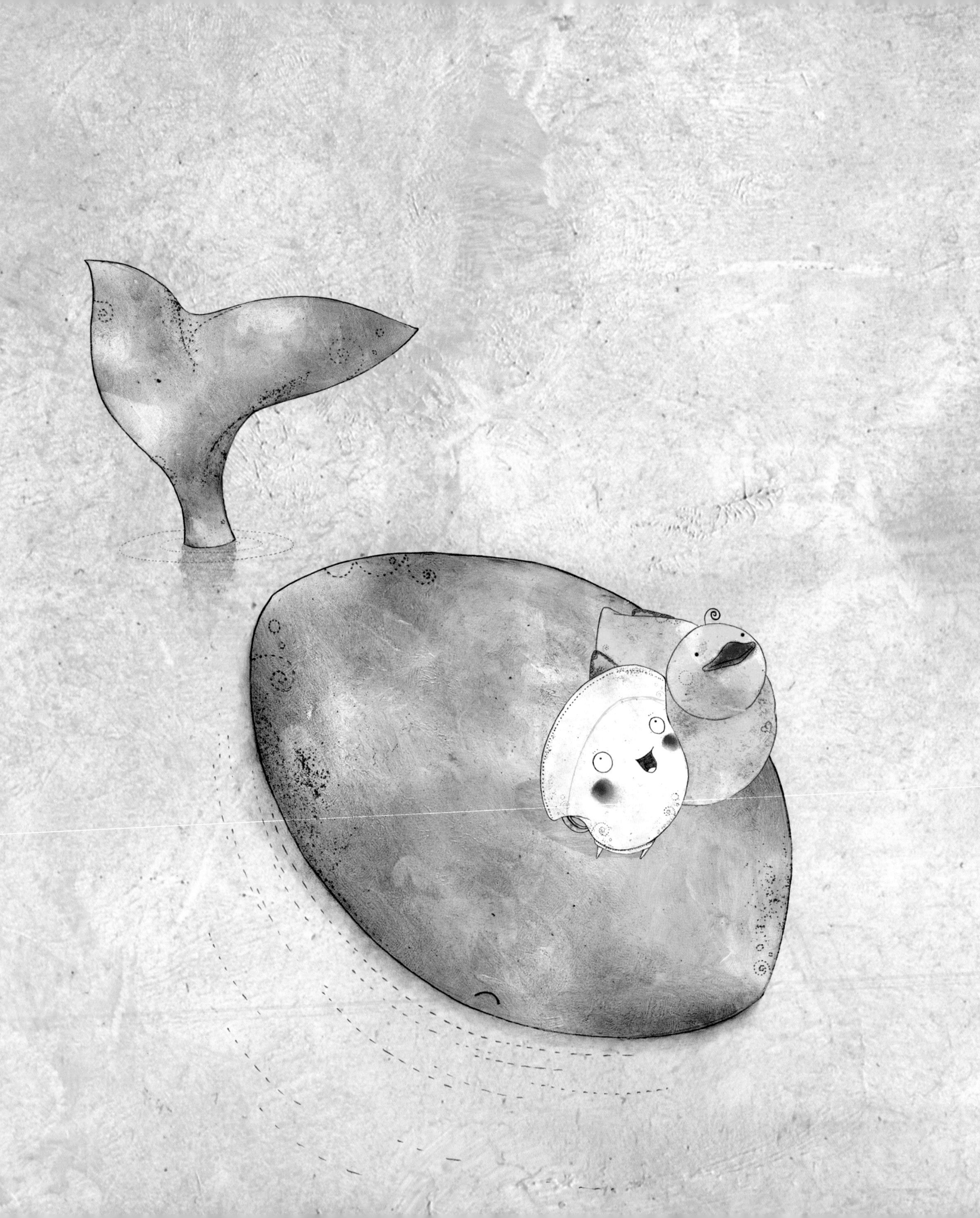

The clouds cleared...

Then the **sun** appeared!

And they could see...

home!

For Mum and Dad

L.M.G.

For Won Hee, who I love most

I.S.N.

First published in 2009
by Meadowside Children's Books
185 Fleet Street London EC4A 2HS
www.meadowsidebooks.com

A CIP catalogue record for this book is available from the British Library

10 9 8 7 6 5 4 3 2 1

Printed in Indonesia